The Dinosaur Who Roared Very LOUD!

Cynthia Hickey

ISBN: 978-1-956654-97-4

Dedicated to Ethan, the cutest little dinosaur!

Ethan lived in a beautiful valley
surrounded by mountains.
His favorite thing to do was
roar really loud and fill the
whole valley with the sound. His
roar carried very far.

But this made the other animals sad.
His loud roar hurt their ears.

"Just because you can roar loud," his mommy said. "Doesn't mean you should. Learn to control your roar. Sometimes danger comes when we make too much noise. God will let you know when to roar."

"Ethan promised to try and went to play hide-n-go seek with his friends.

But he wasn't very good at hiding because he made too much noise.

But one day, the skies began to darken. The dinosaurs grew worried. What would happen to their valley?

Rocks of fire fell from the sky. The ground split.

Ethan's mommy was on the other side of a big split. They were separated!

All of his friends were on the other side, too! Ethan was all alone.

"Come find us," they said. "Pray to God to help."

Ethan didn't roar this time, he cried! Very loud and very long.

But, Ethan's cries drew the attention of a big, mean dinosaur just like his mommy had said. Too much noise was dangerous.

So, Ethan hid and prayed for God to help him not roar.

He stayed hidden until the mean dinosaur went past. Ethan had done it! He'd been quiet while hiding.

By now, nighttime fell. Ethan missed his mommy a lot. Where could she have gone? He set out to find her.

Whenever he saw the mean dinosaur, he held his breath and hid. Was the bad dinosaur going the same way Ethan was?

Ethan walked and walked and walked and didn't see any of his friends or his mommy. He needed to find a way to get over the big divide.

Everywhere that Ethan went, the scary dinosaur followed.

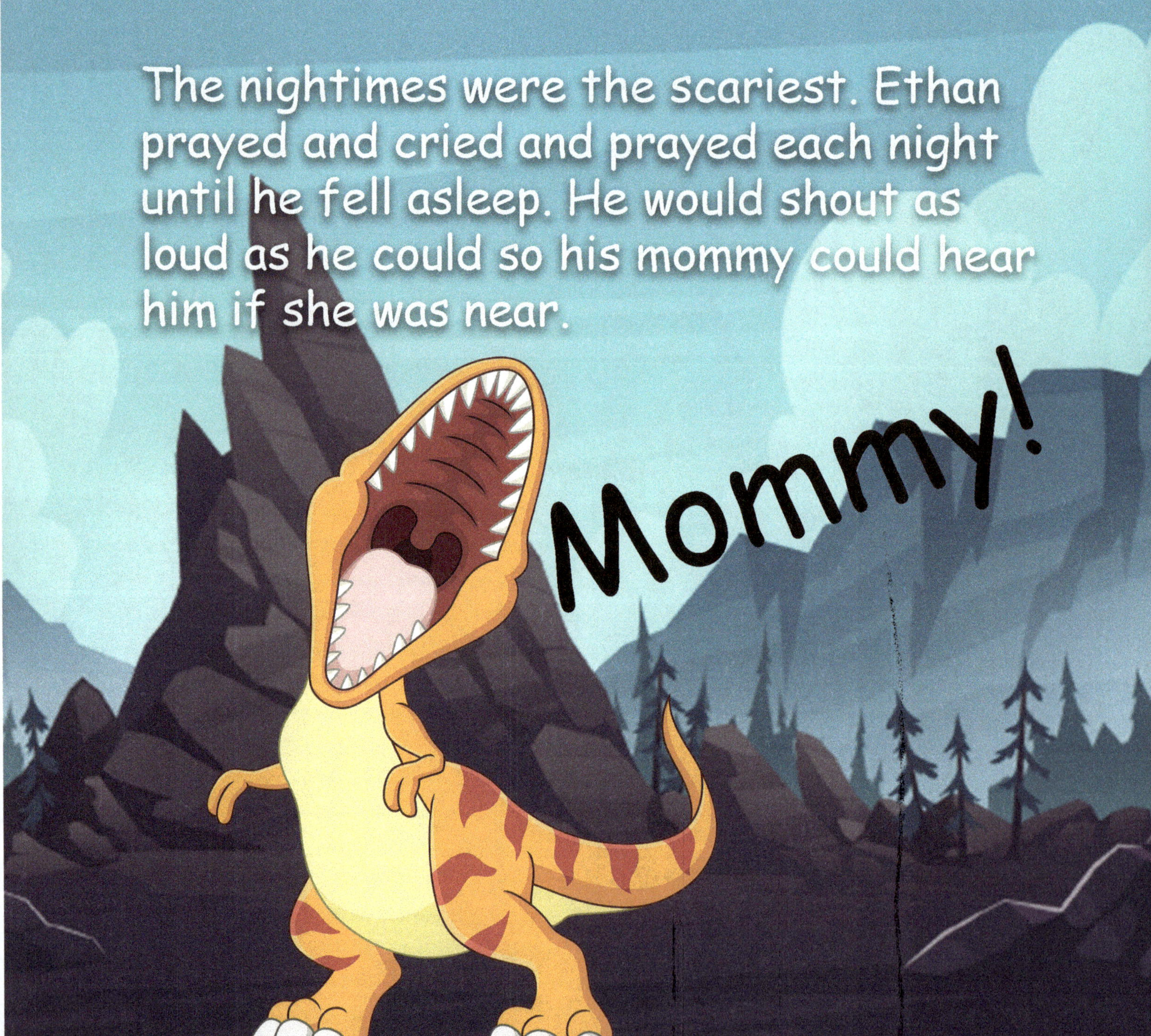

The nightimes were the scariest. Ethan prayed and cried and prayed each night until he fell asleep. He would shout as loud as he could so his mommy could hear him if she was near.

"Yes. May I please go with you? My name is Fred."

Yippee! Ethan wasn't alone anymore. "I'm trying to find my way across the big split. You can help me."

As they continued searching for a way across, Ethan and Fred started to see trees again. Hope leaped in their hearts. They would find their friends and families where there were trees.

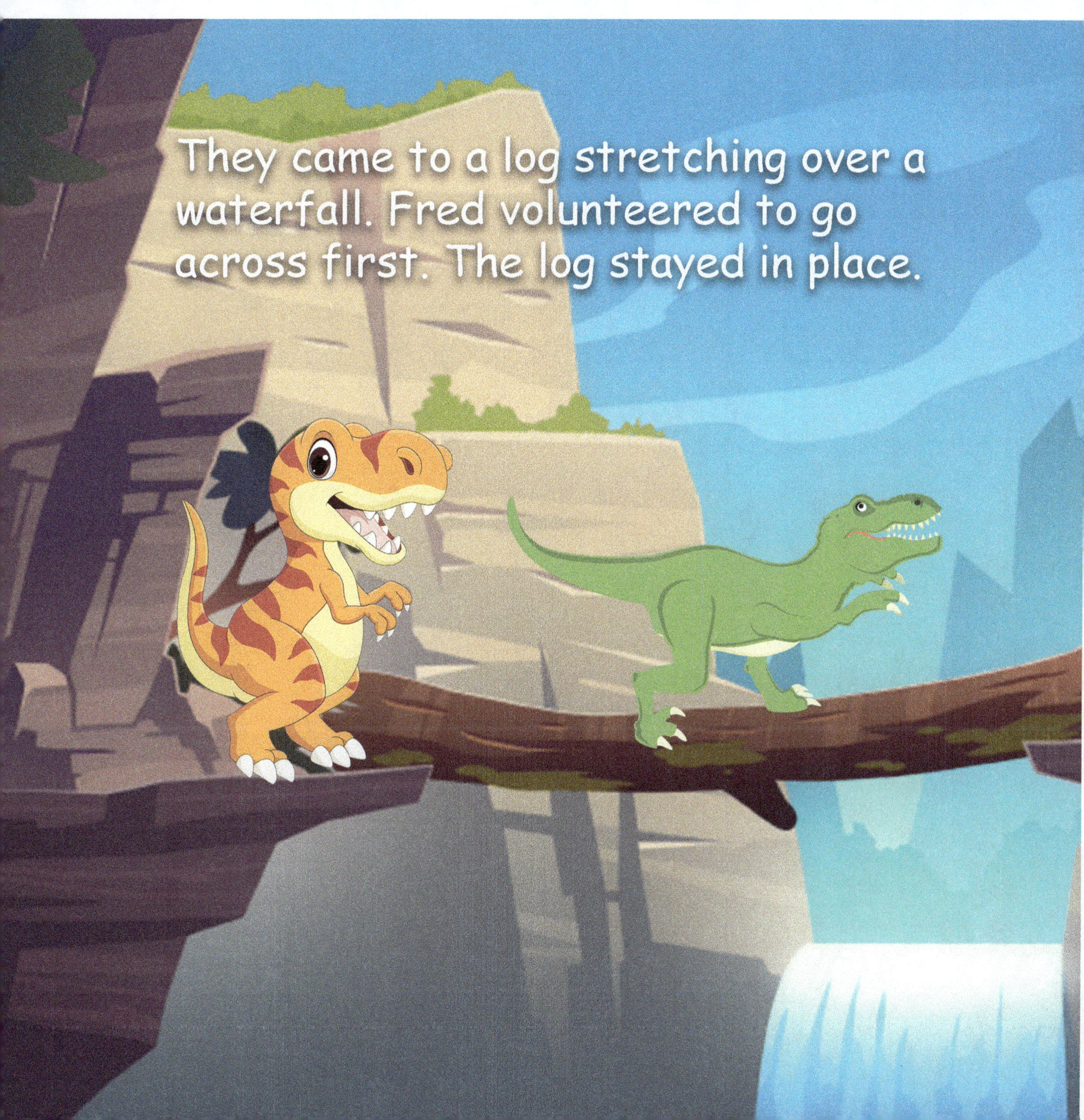
They came to a log stretching over a
waterfall. Fred volunteered to go
across first. The log stayed in place.

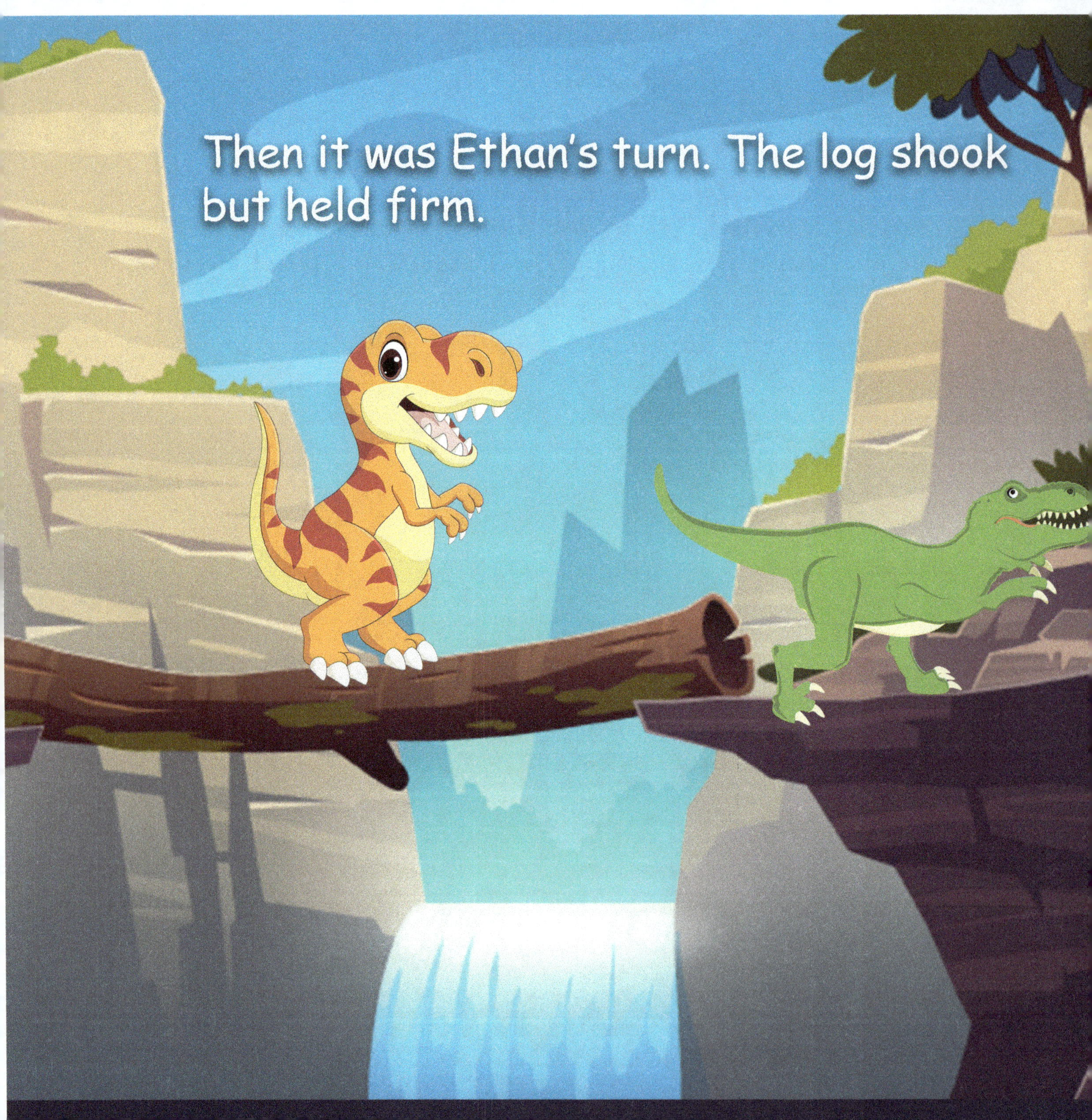
Then it was Ethan's turn. The log shook but held firm.

Soon, they were both safely on the other side of the big divide.

They traveled at night by the light of fireflies.

But Ethan wasn't afraid. He wasn't alone anymore.

Through murky swamps and...

sunshine-filled meadows.

Until one day, Ethan found his mother and friends. He stood tall and proud and roared as loud as he could with great joy! With the help of God and Fred, with some prayer and crying, the lost little dinosaur had found his new home.